Dark Room of the Soul

Rita Morris

BOOK PUBLISHERS NETWORK

Book Publishers Network
P.O. Box 2256
Bothell, WA 98041
Phone: 425.483.3040
www. bookpublishersnetwork.com

Printed in Canada
10 9 8 7 6 5 4 3 2 1

ISBN 978-1-937454-75-3
LCCN 2013933058

Library of Congress Cataloging in Publication

Morris, Rita (Rita Maureen), 1951-

    Darkroom of the soul / Rita Morris. -- Bothell, WA : Book Publishers
Network, c2013.

       p. ; cm.

    ISBN: 978-1-937454-75-3
    Summary: Based on a mandala titled 'A language deeper than
words', each poem-image pair introduces the following sequence,
moving clockwise to expand the circle, and moving deeper into nature
to recover and reveal the forgotten language of the soul.--Publisher.

    1. Nature--Poetry. 2. Nature photography. 3. Spiritual life--Poetry.
4. Soul--Poetry. 5. Human beings--Effect of environment on--Poetry.
6. Feminist spirituality. 7. Mandala. 8. American poetry. I. Title.

PS3613.O77568 D37 2013   2013933058
811/.6--dc23   1307

Cover Designer & Typographer: Chris Burns
Front Cover Photo: Emergence
Back Cover Photos: Left: What Is Stored There   Right: The Howl
www.darkroomofthesoul.com

Dedication

To my family –
Tom, David and Collin

Note on book organization:

The reading of *DarkRoom of the Soul* is based on a mandala titled A Language Deeper Than Words. Each poem-image pair of ALDTW functions to introduce the following sequence of poems and images and moves clockwise, expanding the circle. For the most part, poems are on the left side of the page and images on the right.

Contents

"You must give birth to your images. Fear not the strangeness you feel, the future must enter you……long before it happens."

Rainer Maria Rilke, Poet

I look at my hands…..

impatient in prayer,
so I dream
where my hands cannot go.

Morning's resilience holds
an exotic shimmering in the air.
Droplets anxious to coalesce
hold back their impulse,
wait for the wind to rise fresh.

We had coffee and talked weather
while waiting out the storm,
climbed steps to the deck.
Wind blew sleep awake.

My house begins to sway,
lifted from its foundation
by a pneumatic force
........suspended.......
rising like a white tablecloth,
a rattling of dishes.

The wind pushed waves
to transparency, so thin,
single molecules held
water's shape together.

Through the waves I saw
sunlight motley on the mountains,
emotions shattered on the rocks
in black and white
as on an artist's canvas, not an altar.

At that moment, understanding
stretched and I became aware
of all that has come between us —
drought, doctrines,
delicate and unkind words.

My joy was untroubled
at a nature so vast
I could wake from desire.

1993

What Soul Wants

Her sorry weathered face,
character they call it,
was always as old
as she is now.

No ambition to be noticed,
content to wear her green
and brown dress,
hands extended
to the children.

I dreamed her
dead and buried —
on the headstone, name
divided, Ros—Lyn,

which woke me up
from sleeping my life
away and left to make her
whole in me.

AfterMath

Sept. 11, 2001

It's not yet morning after
my first night here —
moon still in the sky,
mattress on floor
of my old math room
converted to condo.

I spent four years here
exiled from my inner nature
attending classes,
sealing sleep, eyelids.
The Pledge, The Book,
Code of Conduct,
civilized me.

Those years are gone now —
today, my wake up call.
I am once again
a student looking for answers
to a problem
that doesn't add up.

My eyes open as I gaze
out the window
at the pine-studded Ridge
who looks over at me
like Mrs. Plostins who looked
over her classroom,
blackboard behind her.

It's Always First Love

The land seeks me.

Taking the long way round
I return to the place
where it all began
when as a child
I created the path
of remembrance
and return,
immersed in nature's
solitude and seasons,
my first language.

All of memory
from the beginning
lives here.
As red rock belongs
to the mountain
overlooking the river,
and black coal
in the ground below,

so the wind
uplifted by mountains,
slides into town,
wraps itself around me
and pushes
time backward.

Space–Time

The Point

I smiled at a quark today and
       it smiled back.
Enormous in its smallness,
miniscule to ordinary senses
and confined to its wheelchair,
a beleaguered titan rises up before me —
a ripple spreads without limits
in search of bulkhead or beach,
the edge it hopes isn't there.

A quark is 10^{-18} meters in size.

A Language Deeper Than Words

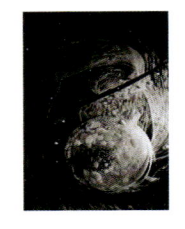

Phases

It was the crescent phase
and advancing absence
that prompted moon's
self-reflection,

concerned about that
growing edge
carved into her.

Those tidal outbursts,
pushing and pulling
made her feel flat,
diminished.

Admittedly,
she saw herself
through another's gaze,
so she fell,

presenting her other side.

The Fall

Questions and Answers

"It is imagination which extends for us the measure of the possible."
Roseau

Rather like a binary computer
questions in life
more often than not
can be reasonably resolved
with a yes or a no
a lot of the time —
our answers plucked from daisies
or the toss of a coin
for an answer which will wear itself out
in all probability.

Where are the limits?
to our questions —
our imaginations
are Richter scales
of great magnitude
extending our senses
to the next decimal place.

All is numbered, weighed, measured,
making something into nothing,
and nothing into something.

Footpath

The Question

The Summons

One Step at a Time

Forking Paths

Blocked

♦ 18 ♦

Release

Shaping

Rest

Those Damn Angels

As we grow older
angelic visions fade,
become deaf
to trills in high C
of bliss unending.

So they take us by surprise
when sublime beauty
reaches the eye —
they are God come
to tell us something.

Outfitted for fantasies,
they unite our dream
and waking worlds
yet remain unfettered,
gilt-winged

no-bodies
drawing us into places
and adventures
at the speed of thought,
sprawling us on our faces.

The Gaze

"You are the image, but I am the frame."
Rainer Maria Rilke

Beholding

Emptiness

Emptiness is a curvature of space
in which your whole body becomes seeing
and recognizes itself deeply.

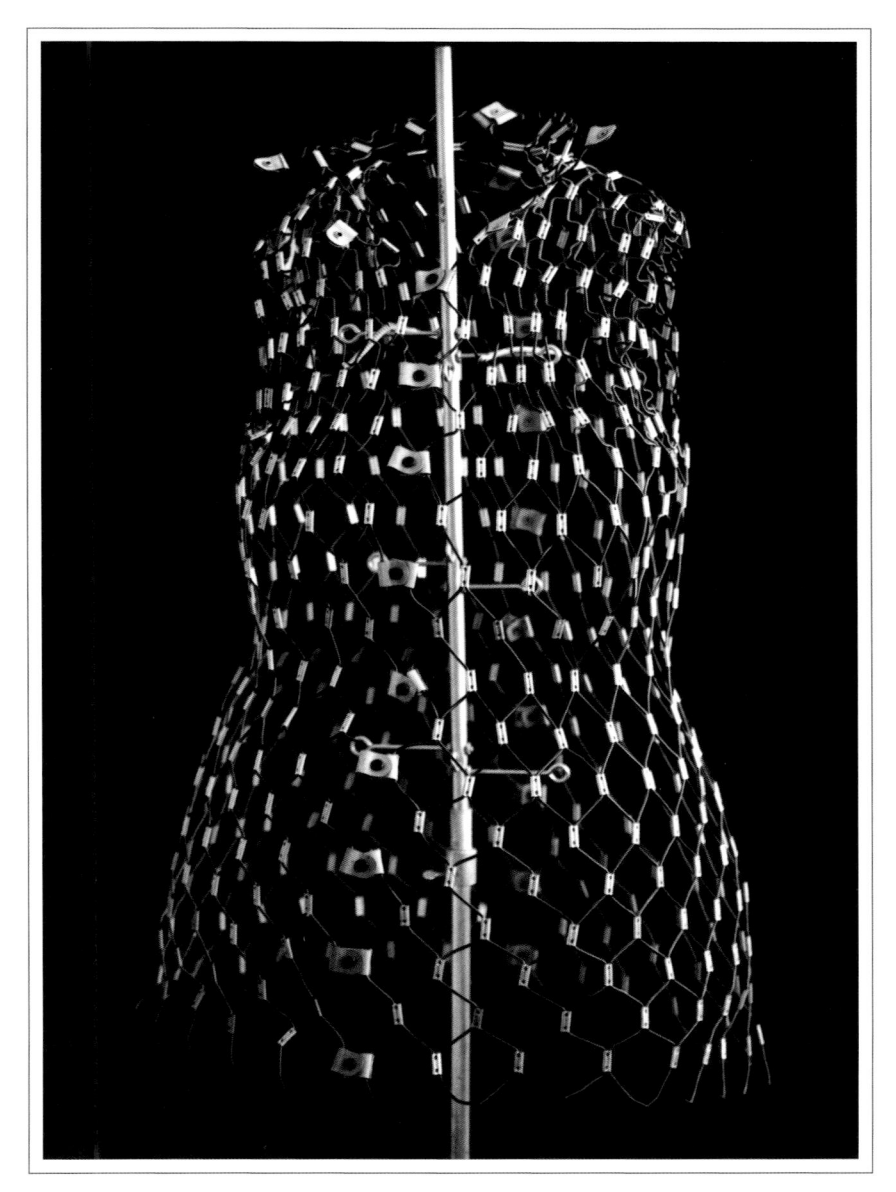

Emptiness

Passion

The sun drops red from the cherry tree
and the body's impulse
ricochets from cell to cell.

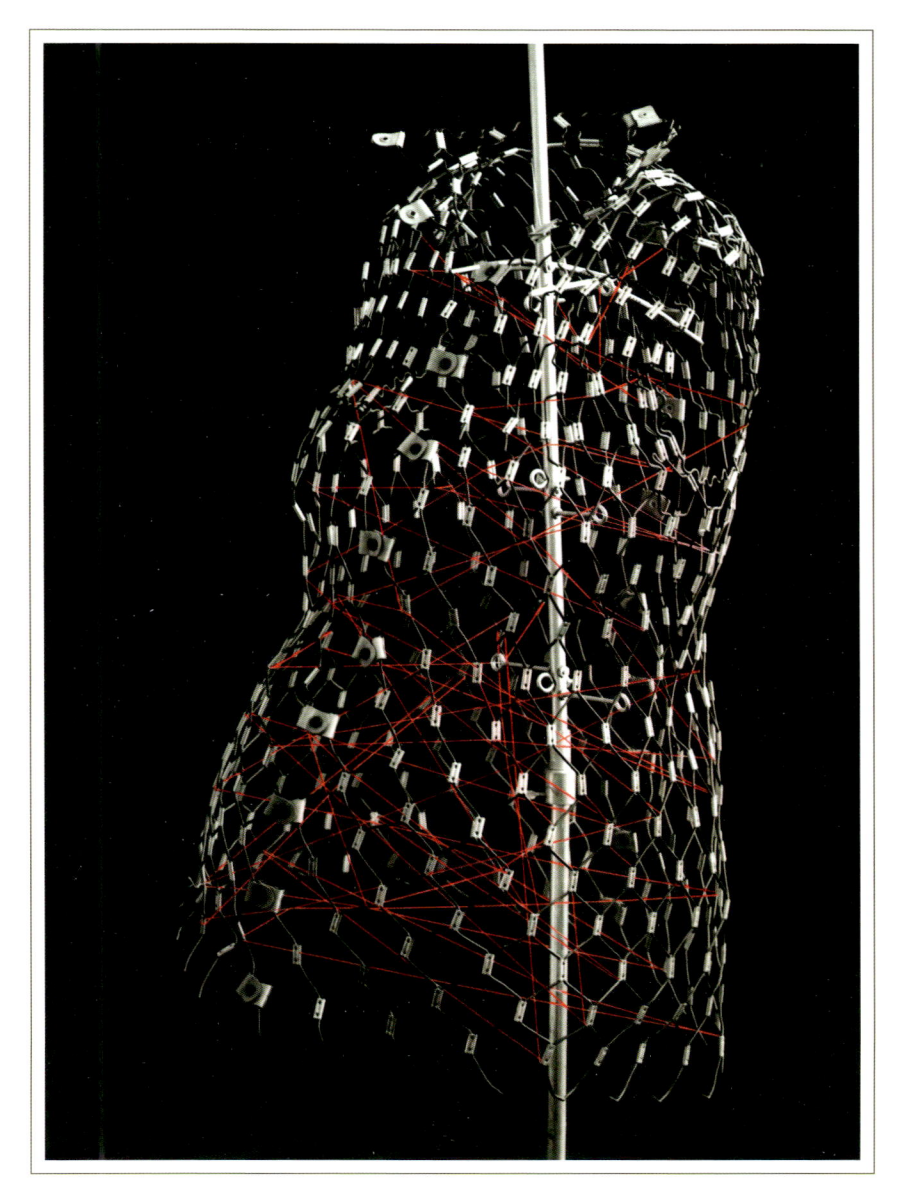

Passion

Compassion

White is silence, the sound
of compassion passing to the inside
while bulging on the outside.

Compassion

Beauty

The garden is gorged with color
and in the middle of all this,
a butterfly tattooed on her breast.

Beauty

The Guild

When skin was paper
and transparency
was not gone
from speech, poets
scraped with a blade
to burnish page flat.

Wrote with sharpened reeds,
wells of ink, (red
for the names of gods),
then erased their words
with ivory horns,

bleeding text
into the layers below,
readying for the next
round of words.

Today's illuminator
straining over old skin
lifts out the line erased,
revealing an older secret
under the new,
releasing images
astonished to be free.

Outside, Looking Up

The Inhabitants

Meeting "Our Lady" on the Highway

My car carries the tension
of indecision —
of driving away from or going to.
This mountain passage
is a border where disputes
mark the lines of strangeness.
Each tree or sagebrush
however contorted
leans to its own side.

A semi behind me,
my car veers
to the left.
Double yellow lines
can't hold me back
and I encounter a place
where deer roam freely
in headlights.

She stretches out her hands
like a hyphenated net
and welcomes me
into her realm
of median yellow.

In that daily ritual of survival
with its accidental crossings
and finding our way back,
we border on each other.

Great Mother

Primitive Child

At times I become a wandering child.
Don't call me homeless,
don't call me wild.

Untangled from the habits
of everyday life – fled
from the paths which before I had tread,

I settle into a room
it's interior black – to reflect
like the moon, inward and back.

My heart no longer tamed
by ferocious civilities – it's pulse
moves by somersaults in my veins.

Dancing Girl

Pop's Claim

As the sun grows
over the summit of Mt. Stuart,
his yearning too, rises
over the ridge of each day
for a shining vault
somewhere thereabouts
in some white-streaked peak
dimmed by scudding vapors.

Curled into the mountain's side
like the chaw stashed
in his whiskered cheek,
glitter waits
to be claimed as ones own —
a short path to riches.

Green granite marks the mother-lode.
"Sham-rock" taunts my mother,
but her perceptions do not reach
him on this spur.
Just another prospector —

like an alpine anemone
which blooms at snow's edge,
petals briefly cupping
that cold glint of sun.

Nonetheless, he ascends
the serpentine course,
drawn by the draft
of a great chimney.

Sol

Lunch

Holy catsup!
Can it be?
A refrigerator full of condiments
and not one slice
of American processed cheese?

Damn!
The cold drapes around my feet.
I close the door,
move back.

My sandwich is loosely
joined together
crust to crust —
a fissure gapes.

I loathe the taste of bread alone.
I hunger for whole, not half.
Where is the missing sun,
bright part of white?

I must find....
Aha....my sweet honey Dijon,
you are mine!

Luna

PMS

The innate tension crests
every 28 days just before
the dam bursts.
My head distended,
my breasts plump
ready to shed.

Is there a path
through this madness?
I've been through this drill before.
Each time, I repeat the pacing,
tolerate the spacing
between words that find their way
out of my body and
into my poems.

Hand held to paper,
unable to release or
contain the pressure,
words drip like a leaky faucet
in direct relation
to the amount of water
retained.

Downflowing

Lips in Place...

I apply suction to the straw
drawing up refreshment
to satisfy an emptiness
that sporadically returns.

Ah, sweet water!
I can hold the soda
s-u-s-p-e-n-d-e-d mid-straw
by placing my tongue
on the tiny orifice
through which it flows.

But when pressure
is released, bubbles
cascade in swift descent
seething with possibilities.

Moments occur
when catalytic feelings
overtake me...
an uncomplimentary
belch breaks through,
carbonated with
creative impulse.

Upwelling

The Significance of Batter

A kitchen is like a pool.
When you go under,
the seamlessness of water
presses its shape against you.
Open your eyes.

Stay calm to the hunger.
This is no time to swallow.
Each morsel could choke you,
each implement kill you.

The important thing is to relax.
Let the weight of routine
and its stubborn daily-ness
hold you up.

Thoughts move as you push them.
Breathe out the stories you don't believe.
Remember, your resistance
is indelible as a laundry pen,
unlike the recipes in your head.

No matter the heat,
the ache in your legs,
the gaping mouths of birds
who perch at the edge,
or the penetrating stain of looks —

learn one thing by heart
when preserving one's life
or baking a cake,
never, ever give up
the bowl...or the batter.

By a Thread

Just Browsing

With unfettered access
to aisles upon aisles of goods,
we meander like corpuscles,
"perfect" strangers enchanted by
    the tumble and hue of fabric,
    the cut and tuck of fashion,
the necessary coordinates
for any occasion.

Down indoor passages
we wander in pilgrimage.
Free-floating desire,
that illusion of pleasure
waits arousal
by posturing models.

The looking ....
is our democratization.
Taking in style at a single glance,
    casually read price tags,
    feign the cool gaze,
that self-absorbed indifference
when we have more time
on our hands than money.

Our leisured access to luxury,
eyes restless and unsatisfied,
allowed to chase that image
we want for ourselves
that gives form to desire —
and resentment —
the final judgment.

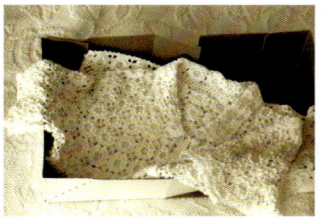

Undressing

Outgrown

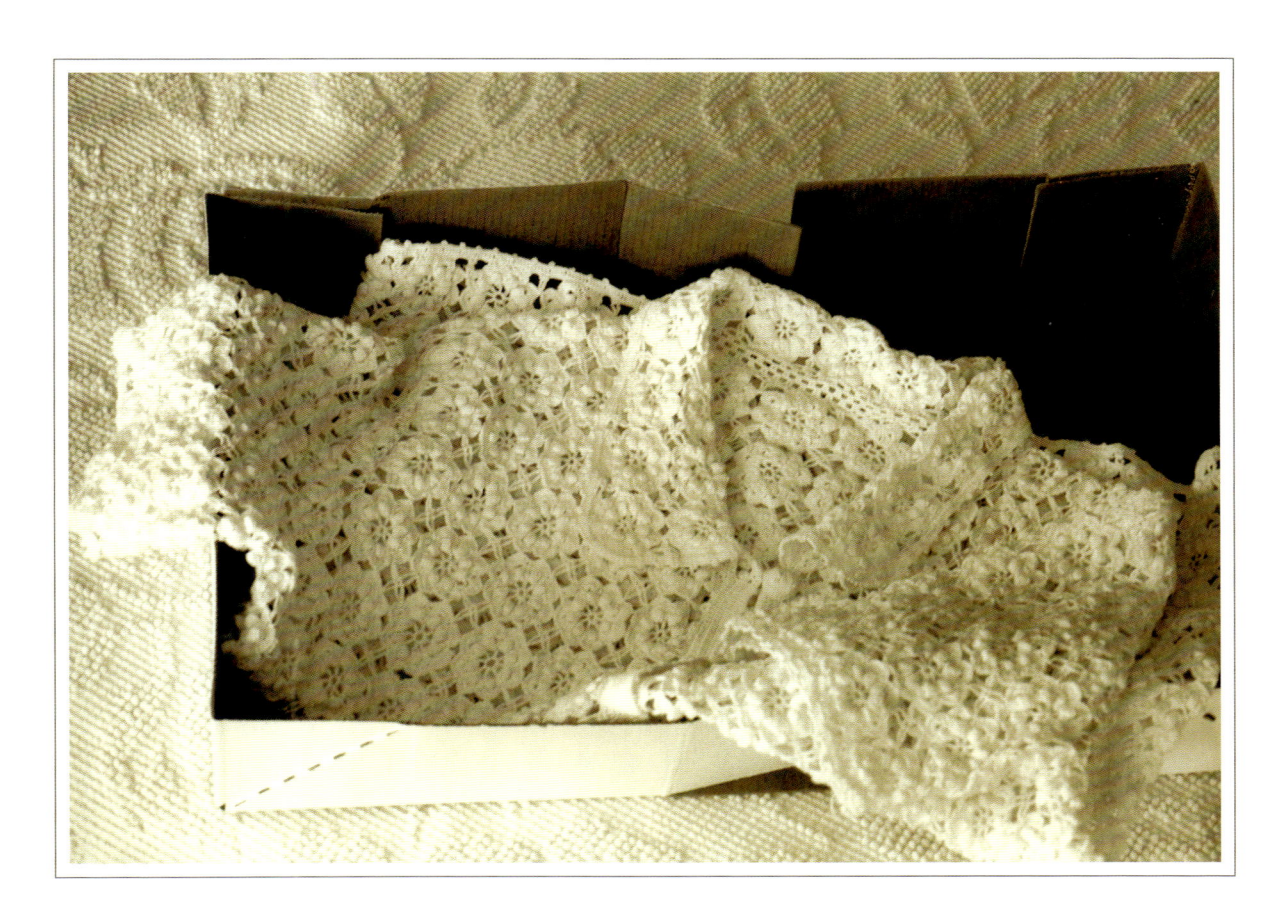

Unfolding

Leaving

♦ 56 ♦

Untied

Unbuttoned

Unseen

Inside-out

Intrusion

Uncovered in dream's kitchen
in pot on stove
a shape-shifting poodle
has been stewing for years.

Pampered, fluffy pet
white, wet,
resenting confinement,
jumps down and
excitedly runs off.

I go downstairs,
accuse the man
of mistreating the dog
but he just continues
playing his cards.

Surfacing

Fresh Rising

I searched for you in form and color.
I called you Father, wind,
son-in-bread,
"green parrot with the red beak". *

I looked for your finger
lit up like a torch
and found instead,
the sanctuary, littered
with sleeping bodies.

Then you came over me
like butter, pulling emotions
to the surface
as from a black hole.

I become smooth, soft,
and malleable
as bread dough rising.

*Soren Kierkegaard

(Read Right to Left)

Water's Dream

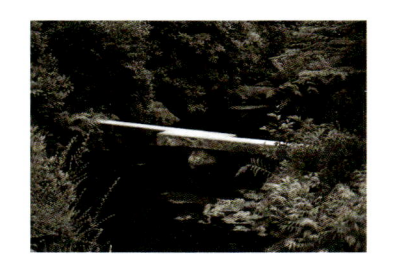

The Shallow End

Overflow

Confluence

Still Water

Raining

The Cauldron

Reflective

The Bridge

"They all shall wax old as a garment; the moths shall eat them up."
Book of Isaiah

Moths

A nest securely tucked
in my head and
camouflaged in gray
attracts moths who eat intelligently
the dark fibers of experience.

Wings relentless,
hitting windows
with no idea that glass is there,
yet always managing
to find their way

into the endless mazes
of my thoughts,
startling light
into the memories I wear.

What Is Stored There

The Descent Begins...

stopping mid-sentence.

Words abandon me,
thoughts in a vacuum
unable to escape in formation.

I grow fiercely weary
in the headwinds, craving
higher altitudes.

I feel the drag of ice,
gravity's unwelcome invitation.
We are not related.

Demagnetized, aimless
as a horizontal nadir
in a world pre-Columbus.

It is easier to laugh, then cry,
than to cry because nothing matters
to laughing because everything matters.

Can you imagine that?

Tracking

The Field

Approaching

On Foot

Dark Woods

Encounter

An Opening

The Pattern

The keys looped up
with each other
cluster in groups.

I try to remove
or realign the keys
in the inseparable ring,

but each is linked
and locked in a loop
without beginning or end.

Can I detach
or break free
from loops captivity?

The Keeper

"I am a little piece of nature." Albert Einstein

Nature's Scaffolding

(Honoring Barbara McClintock,
cytogeneticist, Nobel Laureate in Medicine)

To breed row upon row of uniformity
was the fashion of the day
but a distraction from nature's diversity.
Ciphers of bicolor corn were a text
only she could read.
Each aberrant ear, full and milky
revealed its autobiography in patterns
   of honey and pearl,
    wind bent stalks,
    mottled husks and
    tanned silks.

Not trained to see
beyond her own eyelashes,
she takes an uncharted path,
   her body corn hollow,
    vision impenetrable,
    differences magnified,
finds fine stripes of recessive tissue,
dark spots of dominant order,
ten children each bonded with another
crossing over in games of red rover.

She joins them, running in her sleep.

Tree Sings the Blues

The Ancestors

Young Pine

Conformity

Branching Out

With this Ring

Below

The Fifth Direction

I'm on a train
for a round-trip
to the Copper Canyon,
passing through a landscape
that unravels
and ravels up again,
the deepest labyrinth
in the world.

After flat land
the train ascends
on parallel tracks
that switch-
back and switch-
back again
through the middle
of Mexico.
Eighty times driving into
darkness then popping
out of it
into a new view,
sometimes, caboose over-
passing
engine's gain.
Higher and closer
to the Sun while
at the same time,
closer to the depths
of geologic time.

(Continued on next page)

At the top I look out
through thin air to
canyons ribboned
through rocks,
the high place of
mankind's dawn.
Instincts dwell here still
in caves, children
playing like mountain goats,
always knowing
where the edge
into the void is.

Numberless stars and
moon slice throw light
to feet polished
time-worn paths —
one mis-step and
you fall into nothingness.

Above

The Howl

"How many mouths nature has to fill." John Muir

Logger's Prayer

Oh God of the hills
secreted in all things
evergreen,

as I place these teeth
into your cheek
do not turn away from me.

Don't look to sapphire skies
to rescue you.
I will carve your eulogy
into your heart,

count your rings
and the years
you gave to us,

and let the blessed rain
fall upon your stump.

Tonight, you will mirror the moon!

Second Chance

Designated Development

My mother's arms are uprooted
from her green shoulders,
bushy underarms shaved away
exposing brown skin.

Her sacrifice is everywhere —
rainforests, mountains,
golf courses, highways,
houses too wide and
cities without limits
eclipse her grief.

Another generation passes
as ash rises skyward.
Nature's fury is moving
to your doorstep
demanding civility
from her children.

Dark Song

Grief

Full-Bloom

Energized

Hidden in every atom
of her body
is a nesting power,
tidy, concentrated and
vibrant like a womb.

Surrounded by a galaxy,
a laboring pulse
leaps up and falls
down again,
becoming less rigid
in its boundaries.

In this sheltered place
pumped with energy,
light splays from
her fingertips,
resembling the star
she once was.

Illumination

Sentimental Journeys

(moon landing, July 20th, 1969,
Pinecrest Manor Nursing Home)

Time has wrinkled here,
folded over on itself like aged skin.
I'm washing dishes again,
rinsing off remnants of
grilled cheese and cold sputum,
drying plates sterile.

The residents, saddled
to wheelchairs, hands
clutching controls hidden
in crochet-edged handkerchiefs
maneuver their lunar modules
before their bulbous companion,
the static of dry air
barely able to support sound or life.

Yet, all things are possible in senility.
With wheels locked in place,
there they go again —
gathering moon's treasures
like lovers.

Perennial Moon

Anemones

Cosmos

Hydrangea

Azalea

Pompoms

Magnolia

Dahlias

Daylilies

Snowballs

Wild Rose

Daisies

Rose Bud

Cherry Blossoms

Roses

Star Magnolias

Lilacs

Thunderbird

We drive north to a field
where children peel
from weathered shacks
like lead-based paint,

then converge on us
shouting our names,
riding car bumpers,
cheering and grabbing us.

My arms become feathers with
barbed, giggling quills —
their weight pulling me down,
my weight lifting.

The crafts we brought
are soon exhausted —
friendship bracelets,
balloons blown-up, twisted into
plumed hats for the girls,
blunt swords for the boys.

They steal what they can,
take it into the barn
converted to housing —
red planks, straw, dirt.

Then we get out the parachute,
toss it into the air,
drop to the ground
while it hovers over us
like a giant bird.

We roll in one another,
laughing.

Articulated

One Child

Coming out of shadow,
new moon child
cradles old moon
in her arms.

Secure in her aloneness,
enchanted with earth's offerings,
she shapes a testament
to the sun,

viewing wholeness
through a sliver of light.

Where Will the Children Play?

The Observer

Pine Needle Houses

The pines with gyrating needles
hurl clusters into
the earth like javelins.

Under this scaffold,
children occupy the hills
like settlers, mounding

pine needles into walls,
rooms and houses
without foundation.

Imagination is the house
the child lives in.

Playhouse

Knit and Purl

Hopscotch

The Moment Before

A block from my house
earth's tailings
became dippers for
our bikes to ride
down and up in.

I remember being scared
the first time
hoping the wheels
wouldn't slide out
from under me,
slam into the other side.

An explosion there once
blew ten miners to
kingdom come when
they went down.

No names recalled -
only the laughter above
and below joined
in the moment before,
bridging the distance
between us.

The Dippers

Ripples

To throw flat-bodied stones
over lake's surface
takes precision and aim.

On impact, a hiccup,
then another.
The Moon, sitting
on the edge of her seat,
toes curled,
leans into the leap
to the next
harmonic scale.

Wind, anxious to help,
offers a free ride,
nudging stone along
until it sinks
through a gap

in the water
that gravity has made.

Sticks, Stones and Pinecones

Viewpoint

On this hillside
of shadowed rocks
under jet-streams
and clouds,

I turn on an axis
at the top of the world
on a par with the mountains
that bucket the town.

The creek below
backs up in silence,
flow dammed
by pine branches.

My eyes follow the road
running south from
nature's north, then
meets the highway

going east and west.
The wind shusses
through trees
blowing east.

At this highest and
lowest point of my life
I make a map
to leave this town.

I reach for the crabapples
in my pocket.
They always have
something to say.

Climbing Rocks

Looking Back

It was along one dirt road
stepped into the hillside
that my father took me
in the army jeep and we left
the dog in the dust
as we sped away
no longer able to feed him.

Wheels

Huh!

Silent instrumentalists
sweeten air in the morning.

Buttercups and daffodils
sting seeing.

Clouds stroke sky
to wake her blue.

Grass tests green
her jazz harmonious.

Trillium's gleaming trumpet
mutes its crooning.

Dandelions beckon insects
with undulating yellow.

The scent of lilac brings
inspiration to a crescendo.

Then wind bellows
a fine black dust

sticking to
spring's rising.

Wildflowers

Untied

We grew up together.
Learned lifesaving
by dragging each other
across the pool,
one arm clasped around

the other's neck,
the other arm
pulling water aside,
taking turns pretending
to be dead weight.

Dove for the rock
10 feet deep, too heavy
to be lifted alone,
until we discovered
that if we worked together

we could push it to
the edge of the pool
and pull it up along the wall,
one of us cradling rock,
the other reaching for breath.

Years later, seeing you
on a garden tour,
the inseparableness of arms
and the weight of our lives
pulled us together again and

as before, drifting apart.

The Deep End

Bullfrog Pond

Crowning of the Mushroom Queen

When the last
frost breaks
and lilacs
turn purple,
out of the brown
decaying press
of earth,
a Queen
welcomes those
who come bent
in devotion
looking to find her
sovereign at the base
of the pine
crowning full
in her energy
and dark
lace cap.

Dried Morels

Welcoming The Dark

Dark detours love's sleep
with a message
like shook seltzer —
"Leave light behind."

Unable to be seen
you can hear it in a power outage
in the hum of the transformer
when it blows.

To walk with the dark,
remove the beam
from your eye,
scatter the dust
off your feet,

worship Hermes in secret,
share harsh desires —
hummm...
and grow fat together.

Three Doors

Stranded

Deepening all night
everywhere it lands,
sliding down
deeply angled,
brightly colored
metal roofs
of houses built
with a child's eye in mind.
Concrete steps no longer exist.
In clapboard openings
people stand
blinded at their windows.

Shadow *Lane*

Shadow Lane

Yakama River

Leaving an impatient city
Manuel takes me
back to the natural world,
flat alluvial plains flanked
by arid lavender ridges,
volcanic rich soil
deposited by the Yakama,

sustenance to those who
yield to the seasons.
A cairn of cars set like boulders
encircle the uninvited
camped on its bank,
alternately unpacking and
preparing to leave.

Across the river,
columnar basalt patterned
with red and white polychromes
finger-painted or feathered
by those who came before us.
Nature's stains and shadows
signature their journey.

Pigmented bodies,
the mountain within them
full of its strength
and its fountains, a tiara
sprung from its source.

Note: Manuel Cortez, Pres.,
United Farmworkers of Washington State

Foundation

Friday Night at the Old #3

The valley is veiled
by winter's pallor
obscuring the mines,
repository of an inner black
which time has closed around.

Men go to the tavern
in search of the draught.
Knuckles clutch the bottle,
the same ones used to wrestle
coal to the ground
are smeared black
like their lungs
with memory.

The hours pass.
Fires burn hard and slow.
Men linger over the bar
with open mouths
and white mustaches.

Plumes of smoke
trace the sky,
each belch insistent
as a blackbird whose song
catches in its throat,
trying to find a way out.

Emanations

Echolocation

A freezing night.
A bat, dark smart,
soft brown and seeking heat
is attached to the window
refusing to let go.

Guided through darkness
by unseen forces
come to let me know
that even if I don't know the way
there are others with skills
who will teach me.

The Threshold

Visiting Auntie Emma's

On Sunday mornings
a medley of women would drop by
front door banging,
umbrellas dripping,
their laughter cymbalic,
constant as rain.

I'd slip in through the back,
its green screen opening light
like some prism
into a euphony of color —

aqua   avocado   harvest gold
pale yellow   almond   white
appliances arranged
not to call attention
to their differences.

They poured out black coffee
and stories in voices
reaching back — or looking ahead,
unable to see
what cannot normally be seen
when you enter a rainbow,

how the present eludes you,
slipping further into the rain.

The Yellow Stove

Shaft Street

Finally morning —
breath weakens resolve.
The coffee can on the wood stove
is near dry.
The dog nestles beside it
on brick linoleum
reeking with wood smoke.
My mother in her corrugated robe
prepares corn flakes for breakfast
before leaving for work where
they make heat registers.
My father sweetens his second cup of coffee
with 3 teaspoons of sugar,
evaporated milk and
irritatingly stirs chinks into the air —
I count them.
My feet are propped
on the oven door,
the god of the house,
body hunched over
to hold in its warmth.
The window, flowered with ice
dripping into pools on the sill
frames twin tamaracks
starched white.
An icicle the length of a sword
takes aim from the corner eave,
its blade glistening.

Still Time

The Birds on My Wall

Sulfur-crested cockatoo
embedded in tile
intent on loftier things,
anticipates flight
from kiln's
un-consuming fire.

New World hummingbird
with gyrating wings
captured on blotter paper,
summons nectar
through son's
dexterous fingers.

Bright colored chicken
on dinner platter
gnarled and worn,
not dulled by poverty's
script of affliction,
lifts wings in praise.

My daily reminder
that we all possess wings!

Last Flower Standing

The Butcher Shop

Her nostrils flare at the first scent of "them".

The truck screeches to a halt
in front of the butcher shop,
its bumper crowned
with the head of a 5-point buck
bleeding onto the radiator grill.
Inside the truck's bed,
its hide, already disrobed.

She melts into the tall grass.

They wear brilliant orange caps.
The butcher wears a white apron
and stands in sawdust, his hands vocal.
He splits the carcass,
hangs them on hooks,
like red stalactites they shimmer,
winter fat dripping blood.

She is unable to move her legs.

Working swiftly he takes a knife,
removes bones, sections and
slices muscle into desirable weights,
packages them in waxed white paper,
stamping each with blood-stained thumb.
They load the truck.

She is in their sights. They wave.
She waves back.

Bedroom

St. Teresa Entertains a Frog for Lunch

1. "Come into my room
water-splasher" she greets him
with graciousness depicting
a lady of the cloth.

He, squirming
because of the mud in his eyes
slips into her hand,
green abdomen resting
securely in her palm.

She feeds him flies.
He catches them
with flippant tongue,
wings stuck to his upper lip.

2. My hands though,
capable of other guises
grasps the frog firmly
with one hand
while the other
shoves the probe
down its spinal column,

then, pinned in place,
sturdy hind legs wildly jerk
with each electrical impulse
I apply.

No wonder now,
red-eyed garden friend
that you hide in a sunless place.

Changing Room

A (Dark)Room of My Own

For V. Woolf

For as long as I remember
a wolf has been nipping
at my heels,
hounding me
to make something
of my life.

Whole hours I'll spend
alone in the dark,
casting shadows
on paper boats
that have carried me
to uncharted destinations.

It's always a birthday
party, exposing myself
again and again,
first in silver
then gold.
Nature's mirror outshines me.

The dark is a parallel world
of reflection...
and submersion.

Smoke and Mirrors

Homeless in America

Overproduced, unwanted
like government commodities
shelved in a food bank,
the years make them smaller,
shoulders more rounded,
tucked away with economy of gesture
– same height – same weight –
same gleaming quality.

We look away from the shelves
open to their pain.
Their desire to jump or to hope is
a seal that remains to be broken.
They wait alone.... doze...
looking from the inside out,
beautiful for no one but themselves.

Life can be brutally simple –
an earthquake or flood
is habitually unfair
– we're there –
but these survivors
know waiting and market failure,
hopeful that someone will come
and carry them home in their arms.

Meditation Room

The Secret is Out

"Shall we believe that the soul....is blown away by the winds and perishes as soon as she leaves the body as the world says?"
Socrates, The Phaedo

I'm one of two —

shy bird on a tree branch
in a stained glass window,
bright light shining
through me, looking down

at my rock-body
solidly confused
but still breathing,
though words can't come
without thought
to shape them.

I am sun-woman —
one with the blue sky
and the blue dress
I'm wearing.

The Glass Ceiling

Perseids Showers

Nature's persistence
relies on her habits.
Stars, planets, moons
enfolded in gauze of sky
are constellated
to cycle through time.

But her signature
interests me most —
those bursts of
excitement scribbled
into the night

alive with intent
to create and shape energy
into new forms —
a child's sparkler
hurtling to my waiting
meddling hand.

Octave

A Therapist Visits Job

Smug as a toothache,
Job sits on the dung heap
in devout defiance
letting the dirt in his fist
sift through his bony fingers.

Above him, there is God
with a blue apron tied around his neck
throwing out thoughts
like salt across flour,
a handful of sugar,
a sprinkle of poppy seeds

falls thick and dense as night.
Each breath funnels them in.
Job, always dreaming,
making himself out to be special
sits in analysis
picking seeds out like fleas.

Nothing left to be said,
hand shields his mouth
hiding the evidence
between his teeth.

And Job grew old,
rich and plump
as a roll.

The Crucible

Visiting the Old Neighbors

Hunkered to the hillside
24 cemeteries
hold the graves of
those who got here first —
immigrants from the "Old Country"
who are settled in now,
reminding us of our need
to know them.

The undisputed caretaker
shares with her niece
the Memorial Day ritual
of pulling weeds
and sun-baked grass.
Together they wash
white concrete edgings,
brush moss away
from lettering chiseled
into the gray stones,

shower clumps of
peonies, irises, daffodils.
Their work complete,
proud granite rears over
a garden in bloom
(as if nothing returns
except perennials,
not even the solemn promise
to remember.

Inscriptions

Now I Lay Me Down to Sleep

The Gate

The Way

Holding On

Veil of Tears

Agape

Where Have All the Soldiers Gone?

Grace

The Sweet Here, After

Wild Thing

Rocks in Pantyhose

She endures the swallowing,
the staring to stone,
hands shaping, encasing,
carefully tucking in
each impulse,
instinctual response,
rough edges softened
to a graceful curve.

Passions are easily blurred...
chestnut beige, dusty charcoal
buffed ivory, barely there.
She is blind to their bars.
To escape is illusion —
boundaries secured
by pantyhose and law.

What passes in relationship
is the pleasing grimace
while 'runs' shear the net
releasing her potentials
and stubborn richness.

Emergence

Something Bashful

Remember the miller's daughter
who had until morning
to save her child,
went deep into the woods
looking for a dwarf
muttering Rumpelstilskein.

Remember Eve, hungry for relationship,
climbed a tree and talked to a snake,
shared her knowledge with Adam
sending him into a tailspin
assigning words to things
late into the night.

Remember Coyote, inarticulate,
afraid of that Beaver Wishpoosh
below the lake's surface,
turned to the huckleberry sisters
in his stomach, waiting for a plan
to float to his attention.

Just imagine, each moment
hidden away behind the rattle
of ten thousand words,
something bashful moves —
a new and unpredictable voice
enters the story —
it's what we were longing for.

Secret of the Golden Flowers

Two Buds

Attraction

Union

Two Sides

Separation

Integration

Chemistry

Colorless solutions,
suspended particularity
hidden from view,
an enigma of creation
waiting to be coaxed forth
in precipitating transformations
and careful analysis.

Sleeping Muse, Waking

"If the dream is a translation of the waking life,
waking life is also a translation of the dream."
Rene Magritte

Translations

Return to the Garden

Transference

I enter the garage.
A hummingbird, frantic,
beats its wings
against the window
until it drops
to the sill, exhausted.

I reach to open
the window — it's stuck,
ask it to follow me
as I walk through the door

and from the other side
of the window, say
"you can go now."

It flew out the door
leaving behind
its high-strung-heart
and beating wings
aflutter in my chest.

What Rock Contains

It's 1:30 pm and
a large gray rock
squats in the middle
of the road and as my
car approaches
it cracks open!

Two wings stretch
from fender to fender
lifting itself into the alder.

I stop the car, look up,
find a round face
perched on a branch.

Shoulders square,
its head circles
on a rotating neck
then becomes centered again.

Eyelids scarcely appear
before disappearing
like a camera's shutter.

Next day, its mate
appears same time
repeating the motion
of rock, wings, tree,

watching me watching owl watching me.

Out of Hiding

Guardian of the garden,
four feet of coiled potential
is posed on its belly
beneath the rose bush.

Head lifted slightly,
body hyphenated
with parallel green stripes,
I hurry past and wonder

what brought you
out of hiding
if not to remind me that
what lies beneath
determines the shape
of things to come.

Risk-takers

Two rabbits left behind
after full moon's passing
or exiled from Easter baskets
nibble perennials
near my front door.

Brazenly calling attention
to yourselves, now
sprinting across the road
in front of cars,
mistaking headlights

for the light of the moon.

Coyote Sense

Two coyotes slink
across the lawn,
pausing to look
through the window.

Yes....I realize
two cats and a dog
have provided nourishment.

Once kept separate
we are locked
in this landscape together

since none of us
can be forced
to go against instinct.

I've no pets now,
no grudges.
Keep moving on.

The Compulsion of Ants

Coming in through a crack
between the floor and the wall,
what compelled you
to reveal yourself?

Last time, I fancied
you were the dead
souls of aunts
and we ordered photos
confusion late into the night.

I'll leave you alone.
You know the way out.

HouseCat

Coal black and solitary,
she's in her element now
slouching through tall grass
returned to self-sufficiency.

In my dream you carried
the feisty child outside
by the neck
to learn nature's language.

Later, Bobcat returns
but avoids being seen
moving carefully
from shrub to shrub
tail cropped close.

The Importance of Shelter

A doe birthed a fawn
in the wooded lot next to ours.
As he grew
she stayed close-by,

taught him what to,
what not to eat,
where to find shelter,
how to get around
or leap my fence
for the taste of rose bud.

It's hunting season.
Beside the road
to Salmon la Sac
a herd of deer grazes.

A doe leaves the group,
comes closer until
her gaze meets mine.
It's my neighbor!

Late fall, the young buck
returned home alone.

The Ritual

Just before dark
I go outside, see a hawk
perched on the head
of my owl statue —
"What Nerve!"

Two young ones
sit on the fence
bathing themselves
in the sprinkler
as it pulsates left to right
and back again.

Next day while
picking blueberries,
two shadows swoop down
over my head.
A squirrel flees into the culvert
evading hawks' pursuit.

Mother scolds
from the maple
trying to teach her children
that to prey is to eat.
Nothing sweet about it —
one must be clean,
quick and holy.

Suddenly they're
gone. Hawk's eye
has drawn everything
into itself.

I have been spared
by the winged butchers
but there is blood
on my hands.

A gray bird lies dead
like a stone
on my gray deck —
ritual gift of sacrifice
that I may live.

Adapting

Hearing sounds of knocking
I look for red stain on wood.
Advancing up dead tree
I see woodpecker trying
to find a morsel of nourishment.
Finding nothing, he flies
to another tree.

Uninvited....

...and without social standing,
two large, dark-winged moths
cross mind's boundary
to take on a life of their own.

The first one appeared
next to the sink light.
The other, near the reading light
of my bed. Not welcome!
I tell my husband
to remove them NOW!
which he does. One dies,
the other survives.

It's a mystery of creation
when props intentionally
show up, as my fear
raged from memory

of bedtime when as a child
they came in the evening
beating their wings
against the window until
they found a way in.

What dark thoughts are these
that seek light's company?

The Orca

While I slept,
my two-year-old son
tucked away in his crib
found a blue crayon
and drew a life-size whale
on the wall of his room.
His image caught
everyone's heart.

Beaching itself on the shores
of my dream, a whale
lies sleeping.
I approach without fear
stroking its black-and-white hide,
responding to soul's cry
for someone to love it.

It's graceful awkwardness
plunges me into the depths
where black and white
become one.

Uncertain, whether
to let go
or to stay beside....
in dream, orca returns to the sea,
slipping slowly backwards
into the belly of this poem.

A week later
an orca was found dead
on a Puget Sound beach.

Biomimicry

With an empty day
waiting to be filled
I head out for a walk,
the familiar loop.

Two birch trees beckon,
the only ones around
with leaves
a sparkling percussion.

I smile a greeting
of recognition and
continue my walk,
returning finally
to the trees, now silent.

"Well, are you
just gonna stand there?"
Then they start up again
in an flurry
to some inaudible
soundtrack.

Later, I go shopping for
the tune and knew
that I had found it —
titled "Treetops",
it will have you dancing
till you drop.

The Storm

Black wind of outrage
slaps the walls of my house
submerged in darkness.
Inside, I learn

how to live by candlelight,
watching through skylights
as anguished trees lean into
the relentless assault.

Occasional branches
puncture my eardrums,
impale the lawn.

Hours pass.
Pushing, more pushing
against the giants,
the standing columns.

The torture goes on
until I hear cracking,
then ripping through air
and the final harsh thud.

Black Hen

Grounded now
but not exactly 'chicken'
in the fearful sense,
hen dared to leave
the neighbors' coop
(professor of animal behavior
and psychologist of human nature)
in the middle of winter.

On her own,
days spent dining
on compost, scratching dirt,
and crossing the road
as many times as she pleased.
Nights spent nesting in the woods
plump, satisfied.

Yet, she must have known
those days were limited.
Predators, always patient,
fast for that perfect moment.

The evidence, black feathers.

Red-Tailed Hawk

The hunter has returned.
My husband and son alert me
to this Hermetic figure
vigilant in a tree.

I run downstairs,
press face against window
and at that moment
the fiery messenger
glides slow to the left,

wings stretched broad
as eye meets wild eye
and my featherless
but imaginative soul
feels my own
rust-colored wings
flying by.

Letting Go

A soft spot of desire
grows inside me,
throbs fluid and insistent.

I remember the child
who risked losing his thumb
when he stopped sucking on it.

And the rich young man
wanting happiness
walked away from it,
his riches still his.

and cherries,
dark and sweet, releasing
their bond naturally.

Joy lies at our fingertips
when we loosen our grip.
What remains...
more than our arms can carry.

The Sacrifice

Jane Studies the Hole in the Ozone

See the children play.
A hole over their heads
is cinched tight with a
drawstring.

See the gulls untie
the knots, leaving them
to drift in the wind like
kite-tails.

See blue-charged clouds
fly through the hole
unfurling heat like a
white flag.

See the waves clearly drunk,
stretched out on the sand
as the beach drops away in a
striptease.

See Jane,
the sun through her fingers,
her skin bright as glass.
She too, is losing
density.

The Density of Life

Birth

Little Helper

The Reflection

Down-Cast

♦ 233 ♦

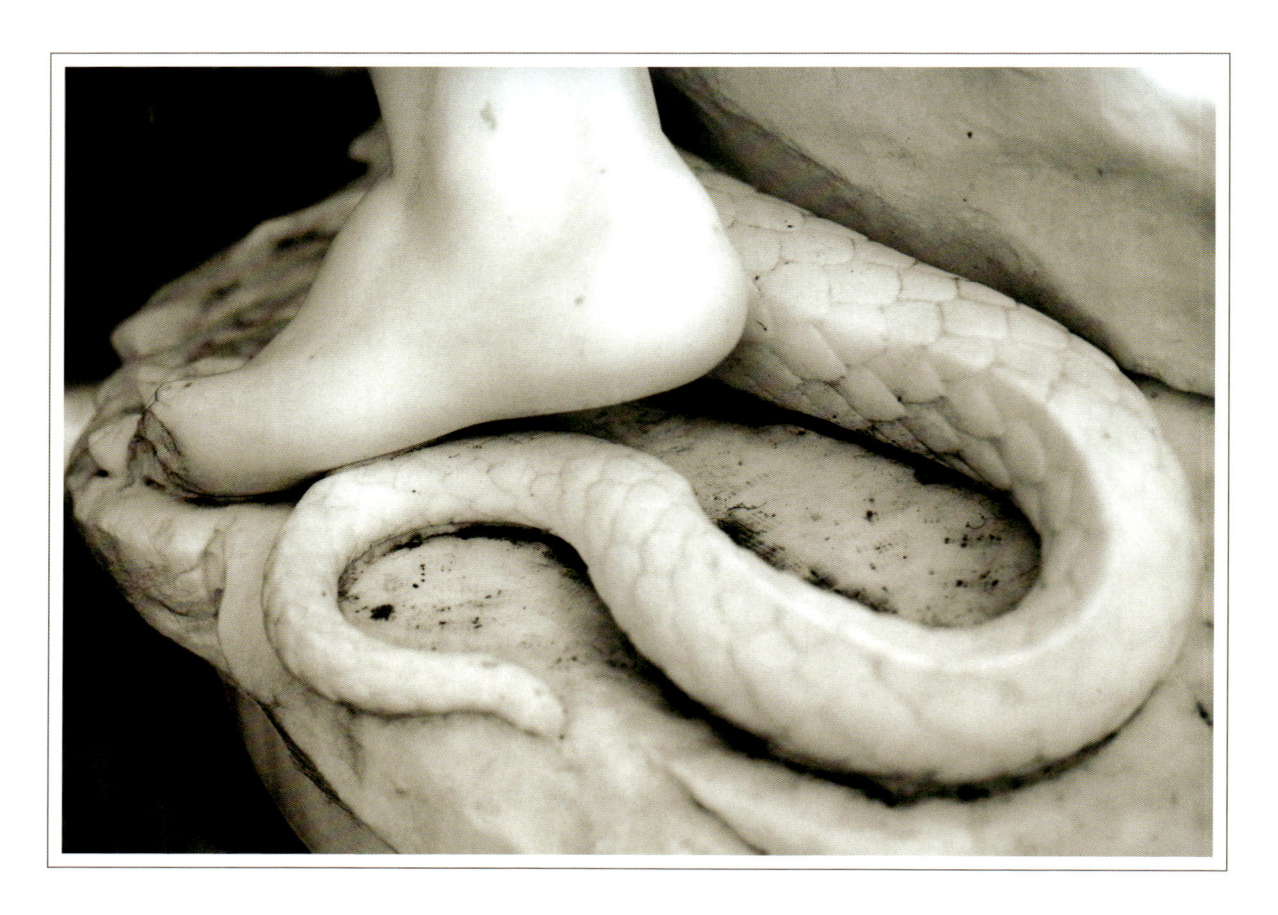

I'm Going Now

On a Pedestal

In His Arms

Hybrid

The Offer

Waiting

Remembering

Recognition

Slivers

1

Not wanting them,
we sow them rich and thick —
send them flying like javelins
into the sky
      where they hover
      unforgiven.

I remember the time
the first astronaut
journeyed farther —
saw swarming slivers afire
sprinkling his metallic encasement —
      a religious event,
      he said.

2

One day, when dusk was near
I spied slivers in the sky —
amber-lit projectiles
available for the taking
      by politicians, gunmen
      and labeling scholars.

Being of sane mind
I stole a sliver from the Gods,
took it into my flesh.

3

To remove a sliver
you must use
a sharp steel needle
to penetrate the wound
      that worries itself deeper
      until identity fades.

Not to remove a sliver
invites pain
or a deep recurring ache.

Heart with Blades

From Scratch

In a world before this one,
rash thoughts
hummed and collided
in random agitation.

Then a finger
poised over the darkness
drew its nail
over this black ground

scratching chaos to sound,
bringing the renting
of pain into the center
of worship.

This too is love —
at times abrasive
as a wool shirt
on a hot summer's day,
or warm and comforting
like woolen socks
on a winter walk.

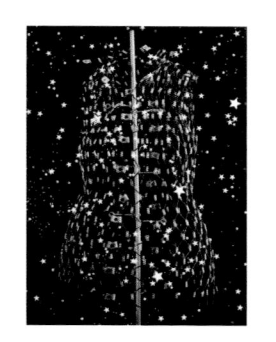
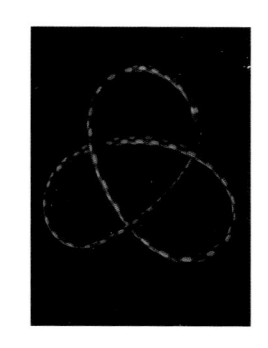
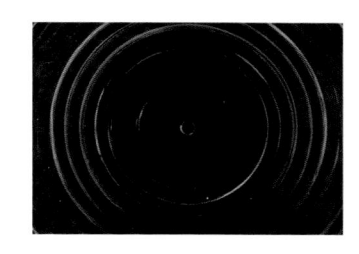

As Above

So Below

"Get three glass eyes;
and, like scurvy politician, seem
to see the things thou dost not."

(King Lear to the Earl of Gloucester)
William Shakespeare

Artificial Eyes

Artists who make eyes
in statues and sculpture
from precious stones or glass
and a beam of light
try to make a meeting place
for your eyes to discover
the one eye that sees you.

Eye/Am

I

The Agreement

Was it an unconscious gesture
or the way she looked at me
when I wrote the question
"do you want to die alone
in your own home?"

that sealed her fate.
I turned away, leaving
her in her last house
where the mind divides itself
to live out her last wish.

I drove blind
into the dark denying sky
across the Columbia and
over Vantage Pass
before I realized
I wasn't alone.

Changing Direction

I dream a larger tree falling
and in its falling,
falls on another smaller tree.

Who holds this falling
in hands that bring
two trees spaced far apart
twogether and
in the bringing, bending?

Spiderwoman

Four wooly brown inches hang
upside down from the ceiling
eyeing me as I shower.

Carefully sliding by
I wonder if can get out
of that seamless net
laid out for me.

I turn towards it
with revenge in my eyes.

Getting to Know You

Weighed down,
my energy sinks
to the first chakra.
I keep silence
while darkness exposes itself
like silver to light.

My decision
is not wholly mine.
Hands pin my wrists
to the bed, holding me
to nature's course.
Acting is out of reach.

Daily I stretch and walk
to ease the pain in my back
while learning surrender
    to path and need,
    to fruit and seed.

In that hollow space above
the smoke detector
there is scratching as with claws,
chewing as with teeth on wires.

Bud and leaf have been stripped
from roses, thorns remain
on naked branches.

I am like my mother's sad
bedraggled cat, curled up
in its litter box waiting to die.

Or the terrified one
hiding under the bed,
forgotten and hungry for days
who anxiously runs to its carrier
when someone stops by.

Against the cloudless sky,
pieces of snake
dangle from blackbird's beak.

The black and white
border collie brings me
the severed head
of a muskrat.

Legend says that
in the beginning, muskrat
dove into primordial waters
bringing soil back,
creating the world.

I bury our heads.

The Art of Detachment

So deep inside,
I am unable to put a lid on
that rim of darkness
I feel trapped in.
Three times I let one
slip through my fingers
and fall on one foot
or the other
stinging its metal into me,
clapping to the floor
and ringing "let go"
until it stops.

Cut the Cord

Sirens

The gray side-by-side
has a voice now.
When the fan gets stuck,
its scream builds to a frenzy
like an air raid in wartime.

Death was imminent.
Even though its brightness still lit up
when we opened it, at night
it wouldn't allow sleep
with its endless screeching
from the inside.

Passing Through

I dream I am in my mother's home
by a window I will open
for a black and yellow
sequined butterfly
coming out of hiding.

Its winged pulse confused
at being lifted out of time
— an opening
that gravity had made

so it could find its way
to the lilacs, where
uplifted shadows gather.

Last Question

I called in the morning
after the dream
but obviously, she didn't hear
what I said when I complained
that I had hurt my back.

She said "You got socks?"
Twice.

First Day of the Week

She had fallen in the bathroom,
a heart attack.
I found a pair of never worn
white socks in a drawer
to wear with her sweats
to bury her in.

'Take off Your Shoes'

You run towards me
and partner my
two block walk
to the mailbox and back.

On point, you dance
around my legs
constantly mewing.
How great, to become
what you loved.

You stop at the end
of the asphalt
while I continue
through the green tunnel
of trees arched over us.

You sit watching me again
as I take leave of you
in your white socks.

All Night, Lightning...

ripped seams into the sky.
Thunder roared through trees
while clouds pelted slivers
to earth without pain,
keeping me awake and saying,

Don't go back to sleep.
Don't go back to sleep.

After-Thought

While reading into the depths
of Borges' poem....

"he happened to look up
and none too soon, beheld
the one thing he left out..."

when movement
catches my eye
and out of thin air
a moth takes form.

Attracted to some critical
corner of my mind
dark-winged shadow
flies toward the light I am.

Successor

I stare hard at the blurred face
in the black reflective surface
of the new refrigerator,
that two-sided monolith
dark outside, light inside
and humming.

Last Sighting

I see framed eyes
between branches
embracing the cedar tree
ascending and descending,
making fun
of the parts you've played
by donning raccoon's mask
for this masquerade.
My eyes follow you
as you slink into the woods.

I I

Who's On Trial?

Courtrooms of the past
tortured the guilty.
Women and the innocent
were sent to jail
or burned —
millions over years
and centuries.

Still today, Justice,
blind-folded during the Renaissance,
remains a woman
whose eyes remain unseen,
unseeing.

Trusting Black

Driving north
snow melt is making
the lake full of itself
after the hardest winter
here in a long time.

At the sno-park
just beyond the lake overlook,
I turn around,
see a black dog
pacing steadily north-bound.

I stop the car,
beckon him towards me
and offer a lift,
return to owner —
reach for his tag
which says
'I'm not lost, I like to wander.
Don't take me with you.
I know the way home.'

Mirroring my limp
from a pinched nerve
he paws back
to the middle of the road
and the hyphenated
yellow line.

A Case of Redress

Green and white floral smock with scooped neck, sleeveless

On my morning walk,
I approach a flock
of long-necked birds
with pink plastic plumage,
each stuck in the lawn
on one leg, swaying
with the wind.

Later,
I enter the courtroom of
right and wrong, decoys
without any depth
of imagination – only facts
are allowed here

to contest a lawyer's fees
and recover the money
she helped herself to while
probating the estate
our mother left us.

A flock of her peers
has landed on the bench
behind me. As their eyes
bore into my back, I recall
my bench-sitting days
at dances.

Tall, tailored, a black shape
enters in black heels
pulling a black suitcase –
documents on wheels.
In step behind her,
a gray dress with elastic waist.

We stand while the judge
in a black robe
softly gathered
at the neck and draped
over his body enters.

The lawyer turns to the judge,
requests a postponement.

Granted. Next case.

Why Justice Was Blind-Folded

Rust colored blouse with black swirling skirt

What a revelation it was
to see seven red-tailed hawks
gathered in one tree
in full leaf, each
on its own branch
waiting for me

to drive against wind's face.
The whole tree
has come home
to nest in me —

claws of vengeance,
flighted scream,
ripping beak and
raucous laugh...
we'll tip the scales
of justice to my side.

We'll surround her
and pluck out those eyes
blind-sighted by money.

She began with lies and heresy,
"Excuse me!" I shrilly exclaim.
Judge says, "Silence? or jail?"

I chose silence.
He rescheduled.

Blind-Sided

Black shirt and black pants

Early morning cold
freezes the pitch
on pinecones
making them drop
like green stones,

ricocheting from branch
to branch as they fall
clacking down the tin
roof of the shed, hitting
the ground hard
like a gavel.

Beneath the surface
of a courtroom lies
a reticent volcano.
Both sides use pressure
hoping for a meltdown.

I think I am dying —
blood pressure up —
pulse fast and breathing shallow,
cold sweat.

She says the facts will show
that she followed all the laws.

The judge orders my
counter-song
be read out loud.
This is good news —
an ancient tactic of purgation
to humiliate criminals
in public.

I retrieve her words
from her labyrinth of paper
and pitched them at her
again and again.
This is your sentence!

There was no meltdown.
She hurried off.

The Judge's decision
came in the mail
and reduced her fees,
but the devil still remained
in the details
of her time-sheet —

if I hired another lawyer
I could nail her to the clock.

Either Justice Had Insight or She Did Not

Black pants and white blouse

Alone with my choice
as night falls, incoming
clouds are dark
from this side.

Then lightning flares,
shocks eyes through blinds,
1, 2, 3 counts later,
thunder groans.

The decision was made
to rest my case.

After court, I approached
the lawyer, stunned
as she turned her back,
walked away from me.

I took off my 'shades',
then asked 'gray'
"Where's my check?"

Let the Curtain Drop

The Intersection

I'm out walking
holding to the center
of the familiar road,
greeting people taking
their dogs for a walk....
mostly poodle breeds
white and curly,
shed-free and
hypoallergenic.

Almost home,
a large black lab
waits on my left, alone
like a freed shadow.
He wags his tail
then walks to the other side
in front of me
and waits —
while I cross over.

As Above, So Below

I I I

"With every death, there is a birth or a marriage." Old saying

The Announcement

I dream a wedding,
a catholic mass
but I haven't met
my future husband.
A black and white minister
will join the two of us
twogether.

Certainty of Desire

Turning left at the intersection
in the church's parking lot,
He waits! Standing bold,
broad shouldered, he beckons
with his antlers — then turns
and bolts. An arrow
penetrates my heart!

Preparations

I've planned a green ceremony
in Marymoor Park. I'll wear
a red-and-black dress, he,
a dark brown suit,
in his antlers, yellow roses
to match my bouquet.

We'll walk from the woods
he shares with the homeless,
take the path along the slough,
our guests on blankets or in trees
will see us through

to the mansion where
our natures will become one
in a golden circle of photographs,
toast our union with pond water,
in which two lotus float.

We'll make history, the two of us,
Hunter and Hunted.

Parallel Paths

I exit the freeway at Marymoor
and at the bottom of the ramp,
I Gasp! at the slumped heap of him
on the shoulder of the road.

His face turned to face the traffic,
hard eyes lifted to the sky,
rack intact, legs splayed out
beneath him while cars

keep coming, helpless
glances turn away from
what is dead inside them
on the shoulder of the road.

We came so close
to joining our natures,
separated long ago
when I was surefooted,
young and bold.

In dream I'm pulled over
by a trooper
and ticketed for speeding.
Then it hit me!
I was the One that killed him.

A Measure of Compliance

In the emergency room
behind the curtain, my body
is a meeting place
for the collision
of hell and paradise.

Perhaps a heart attack or ulcer
was my sacrificial rite.
They checked inside
for what was feeling or
bleeding there —

measured, poked, ultra-sounded,
x-rayed, questioned 'bout
what happened, blood drawn
for enzymes, antibodies,
electrolytes, cell counts,

sent home with pills
to neutralize the rising tide
of what is naked to the eye.

Alchemy of the Body

Wildness is the sadness
that eats away at me.
Unexpressed, it turns
against me, holds
the guilt and anger
as acid, gas and pain.

I fed it pills containing silver,
to stop if skin turns blue.
Another puts out the fire
in hydrogen producing cells.
The third blames bacteria
to spare my innocence,

but I'm a lot like the animal
on the shoulder of the road.

I am Image

A dark spot on X-ray
meant more pictures of my lung
with timed multiple exposures
while moving through
a rotating laser camera.

I waited.....
Dr. on vacation....
clinic's move to new location.

From the woods, barking.
I imagine wolf pacing.
In the sink, a spider.
With the spout I wash it out.

They said it was a benign
calcified granuloma.

Like a dark stone, it lies
behind my heart.

Quickening

Come morning, I felt
a wild radiance hugging
me within, not arms,
but kindness held me,
long-waiting for the time when
we would come full circle,
meet-up once again.

While death may be
the closing hand
that takes back its proposal,
(instead, it was a feast
for blackbird and coyote),

love survived our separation,
crossed time and space
to find us, joining blood,
breath and stone.

Of One Nature

His family stopped by for blueberries
so I went out to greet them.
A Mother, pair of fawns,
the younger, more speckled than the other.

I named them Word and Image
since they're the focus of this story
reflecting back to me
our integration of each other.

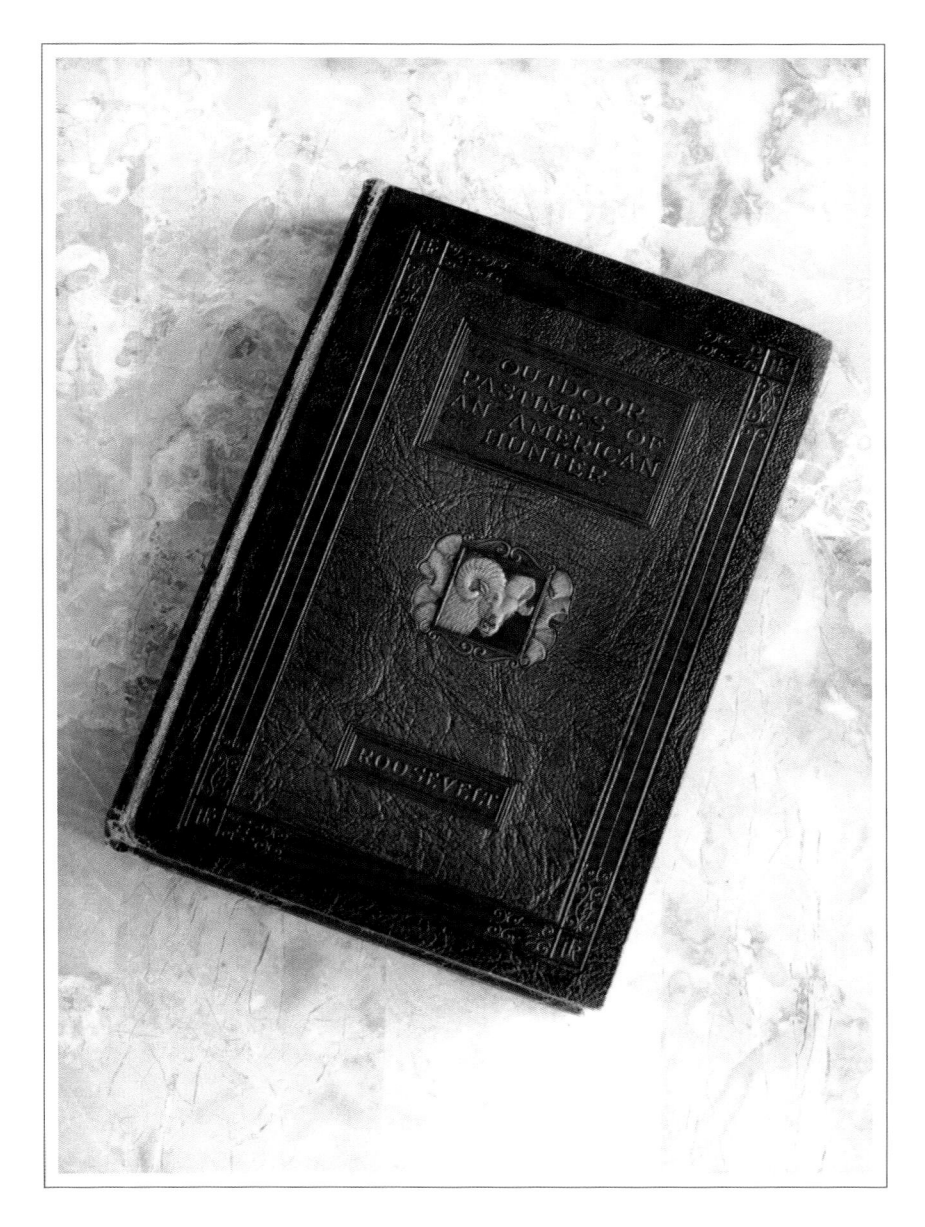

Close the Book

IV

Be Careful What You Wish For

There's no commotion
on the lake now,
but I remember the summer
before high school,
my best friend and I,
intent on swimming
the distance

to the other side,
pushed log to rest on,
way over our heads.
We got half-way
sun setting dark
too late to finish,

when Wishpoosh,
that wily beaver at
the bottom of the lake,
put a wedge between us
and pooshed us apart.

Division hardened
and we went
our separate ways.

The Space Between

The Displacement of Water

Like water which
you can't hold on to,
love recycles without end,
always resurfacing
in another friend.

Again and again
I'd recognize her
like quotation marks
at either end of a sentence,
always a "beginning
and an end" to it
that I'd like to erase.

Yet, in a world that turns
and changes,
if each continues
in opposite directions,
we'll eventually collide or
come back together again.

So images of reunion
overtake memory of
dream, where I'm
standing behind her
at the lunch table
and she doesn't see me.

The Lost Symbol

I watch as she walks
across the street
and enters The Eagles.
I follow. We exchange
smiles, embrace.
It's been 40 years
since our parting and meeting.

I flashback to teeth
behind gun-metal braces
shaping that kill-her smile
when she turned away

and I shuddered,
stared squarely
at the WILD CARD
that fell from the deck –
then laughed!
How 'bout a game?

Like a breeze
she leaves –
being flighty
makes her happy –
but I came here
to dance.

Advice If Drowning

She left her email
so I responded.
Long deliberation
fore-warned messages
between two 'Old Friends'
in a re-match
as memory rose on
ancient defenses.

Lies and forgetting
framed 'so sorry',
'bout Jacks with axes
and Kings who target
practice on heads.

I looked at my hand
— a full house —
but black and red
had switched places.
She says "We'll talk soon."
I folded, game over.

Wishpoosh had me
again, pulling me
down, under,
my body a cauldron
struggling with feeling,
with vision,
left eye blood-shot —
got sick from the spinning
and sinking while holding
breath in.

Then I remembered
my father's advice
from personal experience:
to get out of a whirlpool,
use the sidestroke
and reach for the light.

Getting Even

I'm lying on the couch,
get up and watch
my husband fetch
a ladder, prop it
against a tree,
climb with hacksaw
in hand and cuts off

the branch reaching
too far to one side
over the driveway
seeking light, fresh air.

Don't ! He doesn't hear me.
I watch as it drops,
hits our car, shatters
the windshield,

that bell jar of containment
holding back anger —
that raw, holy, ruthless wind
let loose from culture's grip
of 'just angry over nothing'.
Three times I've swallowed it,
now I'm through with it.

My husband starts the fire.
I tend it, add the branch,
watch anger and desire
become one flame
and burn itself out.

Take-Away

Life's seasonal ritual
opened me up
to the void that shaped
the branches, then
took them away.

I'm used to starting over.
You won't last long
if you can't stand losing.

My roots are still here,
waiting for the next green shoot
to point direction.

Already I feel it within
shaping me, following
its own law, certainties.

No longer the slave
of an eye that
draws anger to itself.

No longer limited
by the bond or the bondage
of reflection, I rest
in the empty space,
no longer masquerading
as matter.

Contrasts

I walk past a window
with a leg lamp in it,
then see them
come down the hill,
turn the corner
and walk in front of me.

Two girls, lock-step
with each other,
talking and laughing –

one blonde and barefoot,
the other, with darker hair
wears practical walking shoes.

A golden retriever
in the middle holds
my two sides
together.

Endings

Her~Me collects images,
prints black and white photographs,
writes poems about dreams
and experiences, so many

to shape into story.
We're equivalents —
joined together
in wildness
and imagination.

Her~Me's language
ends with nature's ending.
Many souls already
extinct, lost forever...

hard to find
in a cultivated world
where nature is not seen
on her own terms.

Silver and gold photos,
soul-full darkrooms,
they too are ending,
silenced — the red light
in the darkroom setting.

This poem is the ending
of Her~Me's story, letting
events play out to their
natural conclusion.

I dream 'Her' death,
losing consciousness
and returning home.
'Her' mother and father,
already dead, greet 'Her'
and want to take a picture.

I force a smile.
Now, it's just Me
and the dog.

V

The Oracle

I see
an older woman
on the sidewalk
walking towards
the intersection
with her two dogs,

both on leashes.
In her right hand
a black lab —
in her left
a white poodle —
pulling her
in opposing directions
but still going forward.

Red Mountain Campground

It was here
I first felt
perception shift,

when strong eye
met clear water
in the presence
of iron mountain.

I descended steps
to river's edge,
watched two ducks
surrender to water's
organic rhythms
riding the current
downstream, until

wind caught their
wings and carried them
up-stream, beyond
where they started.

The Riddle

Eye ready,
I lookabout

until a log
beckons to me —
word and nature
are joined at last!

Four words,
letters shaped from rocks
along log's length —
a greeting
of ceremony and
sacrifice!

Happy B-Day Mel Hole!

The Legend of Mels Hole

Mel's Hole is
a bottomless pit
dead dogs are
dumped into
but its location
remains undisclosed

by Mel Waters
who discovered it
out in the Menashtash
some time ago.

It challenges
immeasurable depths
between here
and there —

a Mount Rainier portal,
or a realm where
ferns harden
to sizzle and burn.

Searching for Answers

For days, I ponder
the hidden meaning
writ there
until I realized
the deeper you go,

down U-turns up.
Clouds part
as I'm carried aloft
no longer subject
to Earth's orbiting pull.

Emptiness
fills me out —
no boundaries,
no need to breathe.

Stars light up
diamond net.

Lightness of Being

The Next Frontier

10. 9. 2009

"If they hunt us
let it be among the stars."
Diane di Prima

Habituated to progress
fueled by lofty ambition,
the hunters looked up
for a target.

Awed by her beauty,
launch pad to planets,
a treasure to mine —
first rocks,
perhaps water.

An unmanned rocket
shot to the moon
triggered the crash
that ears
will not hear, yet
recorded the data
that verified a year later

there was more water
than ever imagined,
when it broke
virgin ground.

The Pattern

Cruel Radiance

12. 21. 2010

Not since 1638
has a lunar eclipse
occurred on the
winter solstice.

Unexpressed,
time waits.....until
nature performs
a balancing act.

I watch as Earth
moves between
sun and moon,
becomes center again

and all are aligned
through the middle.

Overshadowed,
moon reveals herself
in all shades of red —
passion, shame
anger, blood —

the fire one feels
at drive-ins is
one with the fire
melting the ice caps
we could all drown in —

a stunning confusion,
a madness.

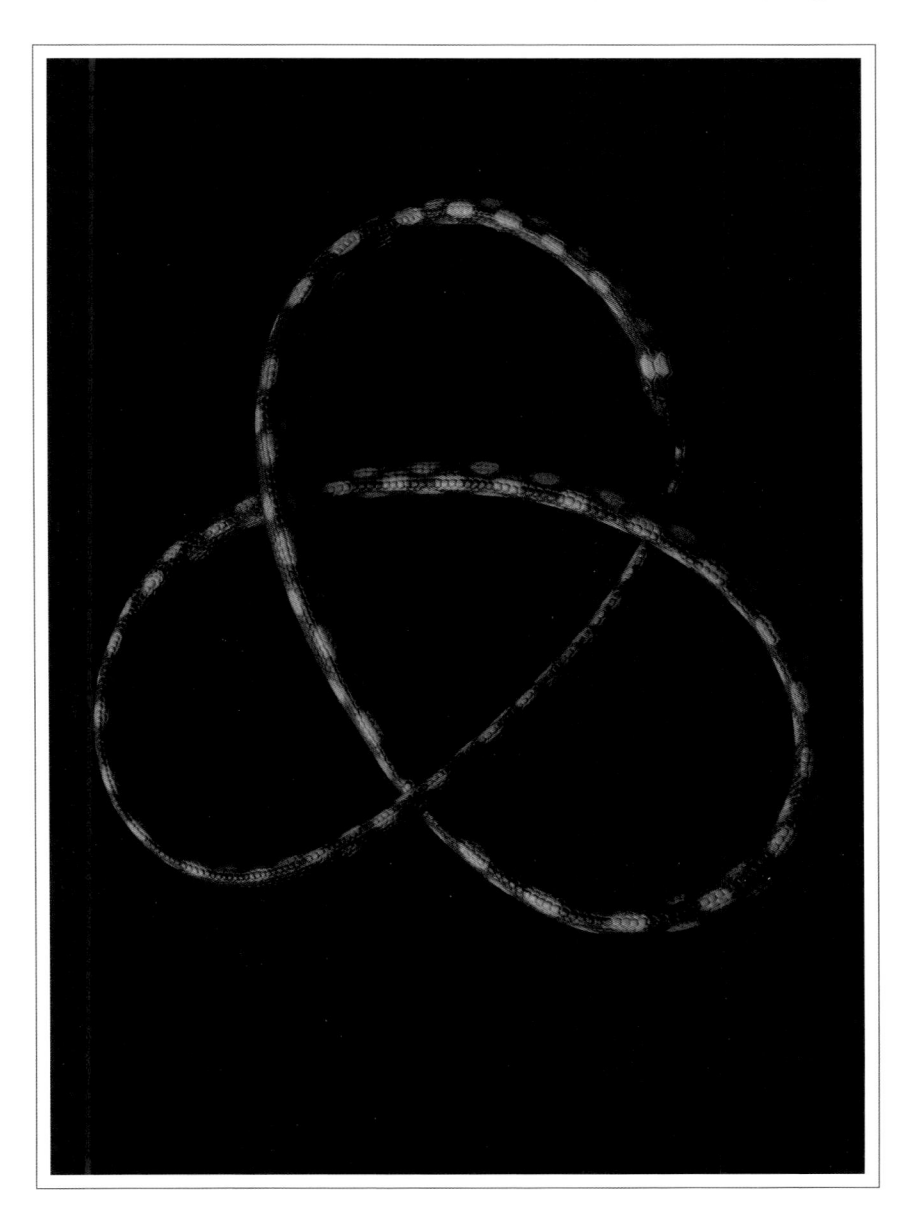

Three is One As the Fourth

All-Seeing

I look down
at moon's dark side
facing me —

behold slivers of light,
circle, and point
has become pupil,

black hole that
joins all things
seen by me.

No beginning,
no ending
to the circle
expanding.

The Dark Side

Brought to the Brink....

of insight and fear,
poetry becomes
necessity like rain
or tears I swallow

to put out the "h"
ignited when
I held back anger's
impulse pushing
those feelings
deeper down in.

Riddle's answer
comes as I write
"Mellow"
with no 'h',
no 'space' between.

I Turn Towards the View

I fall...
like a tree whose roots
have been pulled up
from the ground.

Free to yield,
randomly angled limbs
splay out from me.

Stripped of my bark,
the one fear
I needed to face
was being left behind
for dead.

One learns when
one has fallen....

What Is Required

Standing proud
in front yard
maple tree has spent
it's life responsive
to the seasons,

but it couldn't
re-cover the wound
when bulldozer
scraped its bark away.

Over time,
insects nested,
ate away
its heart of wood,
weakening its ability
to stand up to sudden
southern winds.

But tree made no complaint
when three loggers
brought down crown,
ground up stump,
giving up its life for me.

Now, there's
nothing but

in which to fly.

Three Pair

1

I'm back at lake's edge.

Eleven redneck
turkey vultures
perched in bare tree
wait for me.

I turn around
to photograph
but now, they're
circling above,

inviting me to join
their merry band of
feathered friends,
born to feast
on dead meat.

2

Days later,
black hen has
returned to life again.

I slow.... and stop
while she struts
across the road,
surefooted, cocky,
free.

3

Coming home
I turn into cul de sac.

Owl greets my return
flying right to left
in front of car,
landing on branch.
Eye to level eye
we meet.

She blinks.
I blink back. Then
she flies right and
disappears
on the other side.

Necessary Change

Dream maker extends
a hand, places
a gold coin in mine.

On one side
profile of Lady Liberty —
turned over,
1853,

minted when Washington
became a territory
whose future
contained me.

I am place of my seeking,
ecology of the
soul's imagination
from whose ground
I emerged
and will return.

I am order
1-8-5-3
and freedom
bonded together —
paired sides of
a golden reality.

I Wake...

at the sound
of breaking glass.
Fear of intruders,
stones, enter my thoughts.

At the window I see
nothing but darkness.
I turn on the lights.
Still. No movement,

no shadows.
Then it dawned on me —
silence was broken.

In my night-light
I see earth
suspended in glass
still glistening.

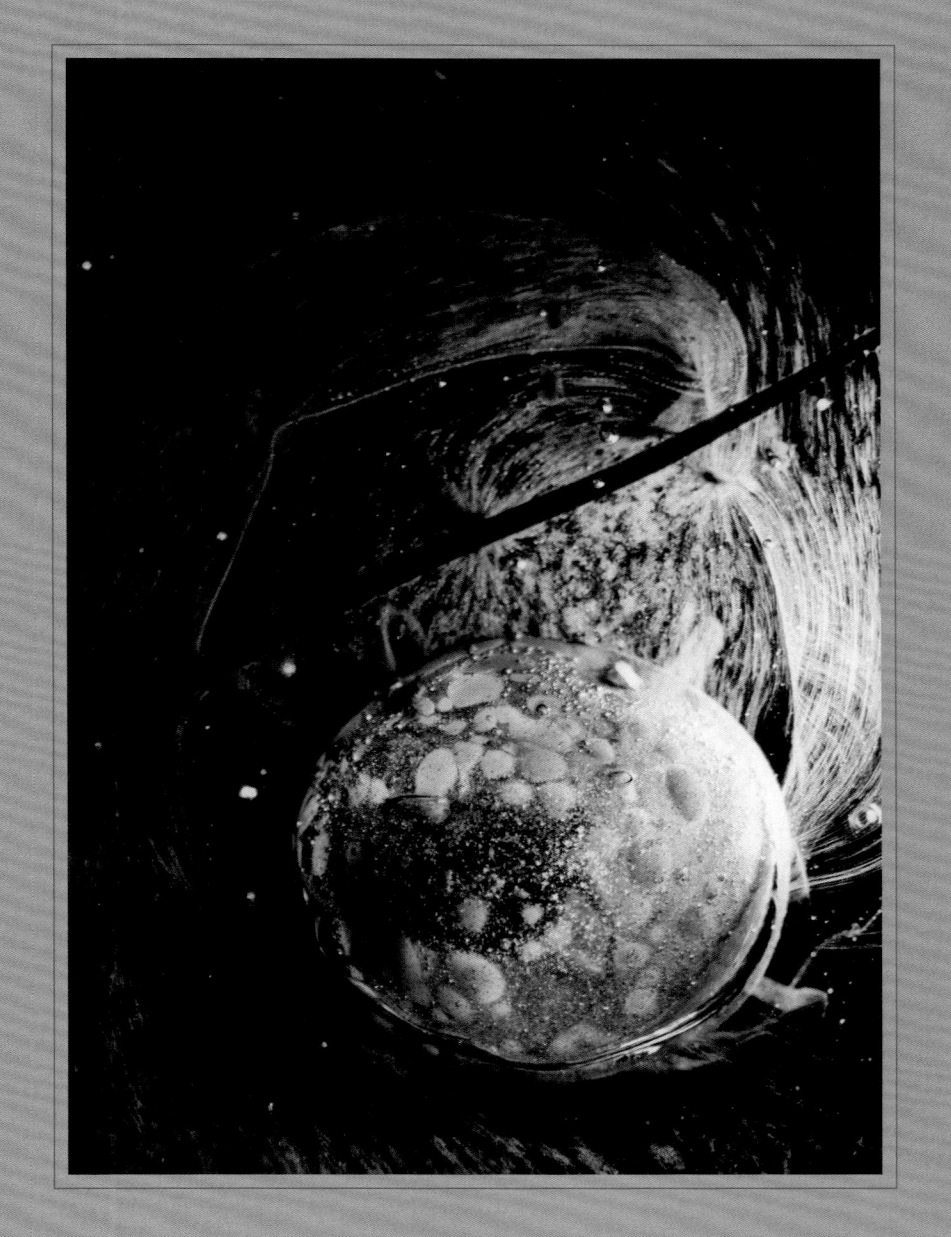

Earth

◆ 307 ◆

Keeping a Promise

Thirty years later,
I, the most prodigal of nieces
am driving to Spokane

to visit my aunt
who was buried there
when she died from cancer
and the interstate iced over,

turning back many
with travel plans
to attend her funeral.

I'm driving the distance
Memorial Day weekend,
held-back tears melting the ice
unattended 'til now.

I place cut perennials
on her green-mowed grave,
yet, a question
remained, "Why here?"

Guided to the South Hill
I enter the garden,
find the fountain without,
the fountain within —

cup of sorrow
and joy of creation,
recycling the water
over and over again.

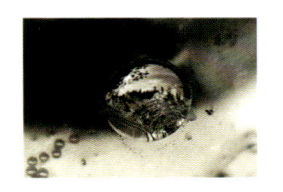

The Fountain

The Aisle

Implicate Order
(with embossed circle, square, triangle)

Time

The Pillar

Uplifting

Joined

Nature, Reflecting on itself

Driving West,

I notice a vehicle
unfathomable
in its blackness
pull up alongside me —
a gas-guzzling van
biggest of its kind,

not a hint of chrome on
body or wheels,
blackout windows.
Its speed matches mine
as we pair the road
for a time.

Suddenly, it picks up
speed, pulls away,
its license plate
proclaiming
this is "REALLY"
the end
of our journey.

◆ 319 ◆

Her Last Words

My brother found the following in a box of his stuff. He gave it to me when I was close to finishing *DarkRoom of the Soul*. It was written in her handwriting.

"Rhythm is evidenced not only on the dance floor but in nature and our bodies as well.

Some common examples that illustrate the concept of rhythm is the act of breathing or the motion of the planets and stars in determining day and night, seasons, years, etc. These are cyclic. Rhythm in dance may also be cyclic or repetitive.

There is order to the way movement is put together to form a dance. A dance if done to music then, is representational of the rhythm of the music."

Rita, age 12

Photographic Processes

Gold-toned silver gelatin prints:
       A Language Deeper Than Words
       The Inhabitants
       The Density of Life
       The Fountain

Warm-sepia toned silver gelatin prints:
       Undressing
       Tree Sings the Blues
       Secret of the Golden Flowers

Handcolored silver gelatin prints (some stamped or embossed):
       Beholding
       Shadow Lane
       One in Where Will the Children Play?

Photopolymer gravure with Charbonnel inks on watercolor paper:
       Where Will the Children Play?

Black and white silver gelatin prints:
       Footpath
       Tracking
       Water's Dream
       Perennial Moon
       Translations
       Inscriptions
       As Above, So Below

All original photographs were printed on fiber paper and processed to archival standards.

Acknowledgments

Heartfelt thanks to the supportive, yet challenging men in my life — my husband and sons, to whom this book is dedicated. And to my two brothers, Jim and Dale Morris, who have always and steadfastly been there for me.

Thank you to my extended family, friends and mentors who have come and gone in my life, each leaving their imprint.

To George Lynn, friend and counselor, many thanks for your kind presence and soulful guidance during my process.

To Jana Harris, my appreciation for your essential editing and poetic recognition.

My heartfelt appreciation to Carol Sund for her business savvy and enduring friendship.

My sincere thanks to Sheryn Hara of Book Publishers Network and Chris Burns, graphic designer, for bringing their magic and craft to *DarkRoom of the Soul.*

I lovingly acknowledge and remember the ancestors of Upper Kittitas County who have taught me much about having roots, embracing place in spite of one's sorrows, and finding joy and solace 'in the hills'.

Grateful acknowledgment is extended to the Northern Kittitas County Historical Society for permission to photograph at the Carpenter House Museum in Cle Elum, WA.

Blessing to Soul who summoned me with beauty and the highest task.

And finally, my gratitude to this beautiful spinning planet and its divine inhabitants who are the best teachers we have.

The following photographs were taken courtesy of the Northern Kittitas County Historical Society at the Carpenter House Museum in Cle Elum, WA. :

Beholding Sequence: Emptiness, Passion, Compassion, Beauty

Undressing Sequence: Outgrown, Unfolding, Leaving, Untied, Unbuttoned, Unseen

Shadow Lane Sequence: The Yellow Stove, Changing Room

As Above, So Below Sequence: Lightness of Being, Close the Book

About the Artist – Rita Morris

A Northwest native, Rita grew up nourished by nature in the small logging and former coal-mining town of Roslyn, Washington in the Cascade Mountains and filming site of the Northern Exposure TV series.

She left Roslyn in 1969 to attend Washington State University, graduated, married and moved to the Seattle area where she worked as a Medical Technologist at several hospitals. While raising two sons, Rita volunteered on issues relating to education and children, war, and farm workers' rights.

Committed to self-expression, Rita's creative outlets have been primarily self-taught, spontaneous, and inner directed. In early 1990 she tried her hand at poetry, then set up a darkroom in 1993. After seven years as a children's portrait photographer, a palpable shift in perception compelled her to express in word and image her soul-connection to Nature.